Look! It's
**Chicken's
sofa!**

PLOP

Is Everyone Ready for FUN?

by Jan Thomas

BEACH LANE BOOKS • New York London Toronto Sydney

It's time to . . .

JUMP!
Up and down,
up and down.

Let's all
JUMP
up and down!

On Chicken's sofa!

Wait a minute! There's no JUMPING on my sofa!

Oh. Okay, Chicken.
We won't JUMP on your sofa anymore.

Is EVERYONE ready for MORE FUN?!

MORE FUN?!

It's time to . . .

DANCE!

Back and forth,
back and forth.

Let's all
DANCE
back and forth!

On Chicken's sofa!

WHAT
are you
doing now?!

You said not to JUMP on your sofa.
We weren't JUMPING.

Is EVERYONE ready for EVEN MORE FUN?!

NO MORE FUN!!

It's time to . . .

WIGGLE!
To and fro,
to and fro.

Let's all
WIGGLE
to and fro!

On Chicken's sofa!

ENOUGH!

There will be no more
JUMPING, DANCING,
or WIGGLING
on my sofa!!

Then there's only one thing left for us to do. . . .

Is EVERYONE ready?

It's time to . . .

NAP!

NAPPING
on my sofa?

yes.